Health AND Fitness

Exercise

A. R. Schaefer

Heinemann Library,
Chicago, IL

www.heinemannraintree.com
Visit our website to find out more information about Heinemann-Raintree books.

To order:

☎ Phone 888-454-2279
💻 Visit www.heinemannraintree.com to browse our catalog and order online.

©2010 Heinemann Library
an imprint of Capstone Global Library, LLC
Chicago, Illinois

Edited by Rebecca Rissman and Catherine Veitch
Designed by Kimberly R. Miracle and Betsy Wernert
Original illustrations © Capstone Global Library Ltd.
Illustrated by Tony Wilson (p9)
Picture research by Elizabeth Alexander
Originated by Dot Gradations Ltd.
Printed in China by South China Printing Company Ltd.

14 13 12 11 10 09
10 9 8 7 6 5 4 3 2 1

Library of Congress Cataloging-in-Publication Data

Schaefer, Adam.
  Exercise / Adam Schaefer.
     p. cm. -- (Health and fitness)
  Includes bibliographical references and index.
  ISBN 978-1-4329-2767-7 (hc) -- ISBN 978-1-4329-2772-1 (pb)
  1. Exercise--Juvenile literature. I. Title.
  RA781.S33 2008
  613.7'1--dc22

                            2008052297

Acknowledgments

We would like to thank the following for permission to reproduce photographs: Alamy pp. **4** (© Andreas Gradin), **19** (© Sally & Richard Greenhill); Corbis pp. **5** (© Michael DeYoung), **12** (© Image Source), **13** (© Tim Pannell), **16** (© Fancy/Veer), **24** (© Tom & Dee Ann McCarthy), **26** (© SW Productions/Brand X), **27** (© LWA-Sharie Kennedy/Zefa); Getty Images pp. **6** (Andrew Olney/Photographer's Choice), **8** (Shannon Fagan/Taxi), **11** (Alistair Berg/Photonica), **25** (Dennis Welsh/UpperCut Images), **29** (Stuart McClymont/Stone); Photolibrary pp. **10** (Paul Paul/F1 Online), **14** Henryk T. Kaiser/Age Fotostock), **15** (Kablonk!), **17** (Plainpicture), **20** & **28** (Corbis), **21** (Juan Silva/Brand X Pictures), **23** (Paul Paul/F1 Online); Rex Features p. **18** (Markku Ulander); Shutterstock p. **22** (© Monkey Business Images).

Cover photograph of a boy playing soccer reproduced with permission of Shutterstock (© Kristian Sekulic).

The publishers would like to thank Yael Biederman for her assistance in the preparation of this book.

Every effort has been made to contact copyright holders of any material reproduced in this book. Any omissions will be rectified in subsequent printings if notice is given to the publisher.

All the Internet addresses (URLs) given in this book were valid at the time of going to press. However, due to the dynamic nature of the Internet, some addresses may have changed, or sites may have changed or ceased to exist since publication. While the author and Publishers regret any inconvenience this may cause readers, no responsibility for any such changes can be accepted by either the author or the Publishers.

Contents

Some words are shown in bold, **like this**. You can find out what they mean by looking in the glossary.

Exercise Keeps Us Healthy

Exercise is an important part of a healthy life. Exercising helps your body and mind to feel good. Also, exercise can be fun.

Exercising with friends is fun!

Riding a bicycle is a good way to exercise.

You are exercising when you ride your bike. Playing tag or chase is an easy way to exercise. Even planting a garden is good exercise for your body.

What Is Exercise?

Your Choice:

You like playing computer games indoors. You have a soccer computer game that is fun to play. Is that good exercise?

Computer games are fun but are they exercise?

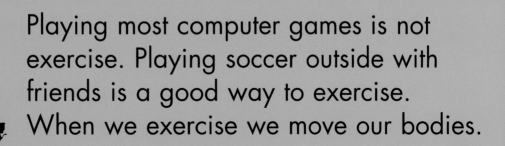

Playing most computer games is not exercise. Playing soccer outside with friends is a good way to exercise. When we exercise we move our bodies.

Thirty minutes of cycling is about equal to:

 10 minutes fast running

 34 minutes volleyball

 11 minutes rollerblading

 36 minutes fast walking

 17 minutes playing tennis or jogging (slow running)

 54 minutes slow walking

 19 minutes swimming

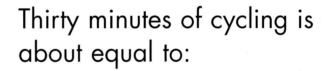

Exercise Your Whole Body

Most games and sports are good for your whole body. Different kinds of exercise are good for some parts of your body. For example, swimming makes your arms strong, while running is good for your leg **muscles**.

Climbing helps to build strong leg and arm muscles.

The muscles of the body

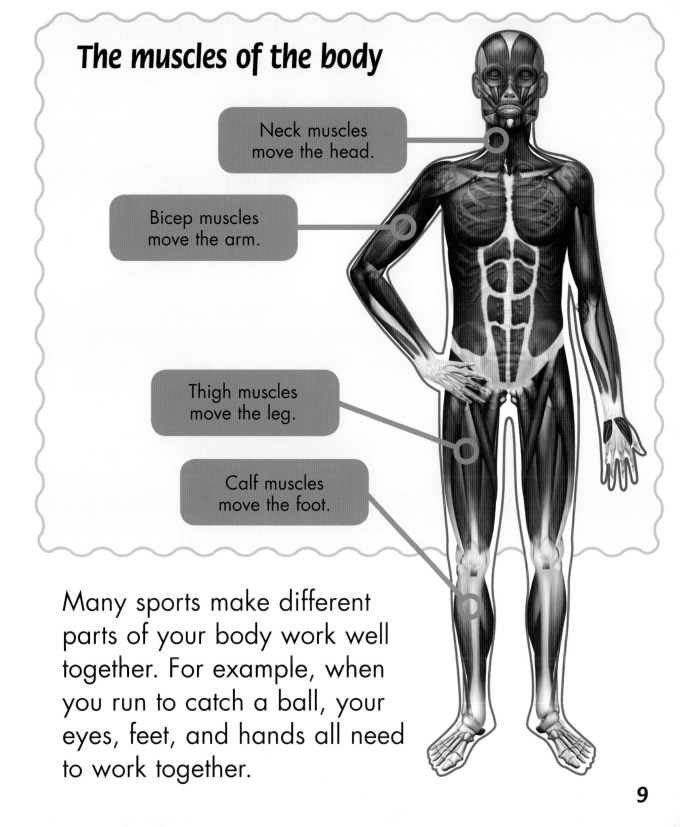

Neck muscles move the head.

Bicep muscles move the arm.

Thigh muscles move the leg.

Calf muscles move the foot.

Many sports make different parts of your body work well together. For example, when you run to catch a ball, your eyes, feet, and hands all need to work together.

Exercise Your Heart and Lungs

These children's hearts are pumping blood to all parts of their bodies.

Exercising makes you breathe more quickly and makes your **heart** beat faster. This makes your blood move **oxygen** from your **lungs** around your body. The different parts of your body need oxygen to work well.

We exercise our hearts
and lungs when we run.

To strengthen your heart and lungs, it is
important to exercise every day. You should
try to make your heart beat fast for an hour
almost every day.

Exercise Your Muscles and Bones

Games or exercise make your **muscles** work. It is good for muscles to work hard and get stronger. Muscles help your bones move.

Doing pull-ups makes your arm and back muscles strong.

Milk also helps keep your bones healthy.

Every time you lift, stretch, or bend you are using muscles. Almost all exercise will make your muscles or bones stronger. Swimming, jumping jacks, and climbing stairs are all good exercise.

Exercise Your Brain and Mind

Exercise will make your **heart** beat faster. Your heart pumps **oxygen** around your body. When your heart beats fast, it will pump more oxygen to your **brain**.

Physical exercise makes you feel good.

Oxygen helps your brain to work well, so you can think quickly and clearly. Exercise helps you **concentrate** in school. It is also a great way to make friends.

These children are having a good time exercising together.

Safe Places to Exercise

Your Choice:

You want to play a game of soccer with your friends. Is the street a good place to play?

It is important to exercise in a safe place.

Look out for **hazards** like broken glass where you play.

The street can be a dangerous place to play. Stay away from any broken glass and moving cars or other traffic, including bicycles. It is better to find a safe place to play and exercise.

Exercising at School

Most children can exercise at school. PE is a class where you can be active. Playing games, exercising, and dancing can all be part of PE.

Moving around during PE can be a good break from sitting in the classroom.

Running races is a good way to spend recess.

Recess is another time when you can exercise. You should try to exercise when you are out for recess every day. Walking or cycling to school is also a good way to get exercise.

Exercising at Home

Your choice:

A parent asks you to help in the garden. They want you to pull weeds and do some raking. Is that exercise?

Exercise can be more than just games.

20

Doing work inside or outside can be good exercise. Working in the garden makes your back and legs strong. Helping carry groceries or doing chores in the house works the **muscles** in your arms.

It is possible to exercise in many different ways.

Exercising by Yourself

Flying a kite is a great way to exercise.

There are many ways to exercise on your own. You could ride a bicycle, jog, or practice your favorite sport. It can be a good time to think or **relax**.

Doing sit-ups or rollerblading are more good ways to exercise by yourself. You should always make sure an adult knows what you are doing.

Exercising near adults is a good way to stay safe.

Exercising with Others

Team sports are one way to exercise with others. Basketball and soccer are sports to play with a group of friends.

Running around a basketball court is good for your **lungs** and **heart**.

Exercising with someone else can be safer and more fun than exercising alone.

Sports are one way to exercise, but you can also do an **activity** with friends. Riding bikes, playing tag, going for a walk, and swimming are all good exercise.

Too Much Exercise?

Your Choice:

Some exercise is good for your body. Is it a good idea to exercise all the time?

It is a good idea to stretch before and after exercise.

Your body needs time to rest, too. Exercise a few times a week and always stop if it hurts. Exercise should be fun and feel good.

Always try to rest after exercise.

Exercising for a Lifetime

Exercise is important for adults as well as children. When people get older, their lives can get busy. They still need to exercise a little every day.

It only takes a few minutes a day to get enough exercise.

Exercise is an important part of a healthy life. Start exercising now and you will have a good **habit** for the rest of your life.

Exercise can be fun at any age.

Glossary

activity something you do

brain part of your body that helps you think, remember, feel, and move

concentrate when you think hard about what you are doing

habit thing you do often

hazard danger. Hazards are things to be careful around.

heart part of your body that pumps blood all around the rest of your body

lung part of your body that helps you breathe in and out

muscle part of your body that can help your bones move

oxygen part of the air that we need to live

relax rest

team group of people

Find Out More

Books to Read

Gogerly, Liz. *Exercise*. New York: Crabtree, 2008.

Gray, Shirley W. *Exercising for Good Health*. Chanhassen, Minn.: Child's World, 2004.

Royston, Angela. *Get Some Exercise!*. Chicago: Heinemann Library, 2004.

Royston, Angela. *Why Do We Need To Be Active?*. Chicago: Heinemann Library, 2005.

Salzmann, Mary Elizabeth. *Being Active*. Edina, Minn.: Abdo Pub., 2004.

Tourville, Amanda Doering. *Get Up and Go: Being Active*. Minneapolis, Minn.: Picture Window Books, 2008.

Websites

http://kidshealth.org/kid/exercise/fit/work_it_out.html
Find out why exercise is cool.

Index